UNDEAD PETS

NIGHT OF THE HOWLING HOUND

SAM HAY

ILLUSTRATED BY SIMON COOPER

Stripes

The story so far...

Ten-year-old
Joe Edmunds is
desperate for a pet.

But his mum's allergies mean
that he's got no chance.

Then his great-uncle
Charlie gives him an
ancient Egyptian amulet
that he claims will grant
Joe a single wish...

UNDEAD PETS

NIGHT OF THE HOWLING HOUND

For Ja – SH

This one's for Evie Cleevie – SC

STRIPES PUBLISHING
An imprint of Little Tiger Press
1 The Coda Centre, 189 Munster Road,
London SW6 6AW

A paperback original
First published in Great Britain in 2013

Text copyright © Sam Hay, 2013
Illustrations copyright © Simon Cooper, 2013

ISBN: 978-1-84715-362-3

The right of Sam Hay and Simon Cooper to be identified as the author
and illustrator of this work respectively has been asserted by them in
accordance with the Copyright, Designs and Patents Act, 1988.

A CIP catalogue record for this book is available from
the British Library.

Printed and bound in the UK.
10 9 8 7 6 5 4 3 2 1

But instead of getting a pet, Joe becomes the Protector of Undead Pets. He is bound by the amulet to solve the problems of zombie pets so they can pass peacefully to the afterlife.

And so the trouble begins...

Wolf's Leap
ACTIVITY CENTRE

CHAPTER ONE

THWACK!

Joe gave the tent peg a thump with the mallet, then tugged the rope to make sure it was secure.

"Awesome!" said Matt, who was pegging in the other side. "Looks like we're the first to finish!"

They were at the Wolf's Leap Activity Centre on the edge of Brockton Forest for a school camping trip.

"Not even a tornado would shift this thing!" said Ben, poking his head out of the tent.

Undead Pets

But just then a tornado did shift it; a tornado in the shape of Bradley Piker, or Spiker, as he was known. He raced over, and hurled himself at the side of the tent, making it bulge inwards.

"Hey!" yelled Joe. "Watch it!"

"Says who? This is my tent, too," said Spiker. "I'm in with you guys tonight!"

"What?" Joe groaned. He really didn't want to share a tent with Spiker – he was the gobbiest trouble-maker in the class.

"Yep! Mr Hill says I'm with you. I hope you're not going to wet your pants and call for your mummy when it gets dark tonight, Joe Edmunds!"

Joe shot him a dirty look.

"Especially if the wolf starts howling," smirked Spiker. "The ghost wolf of Brockton Forest…"

"Yeah, yeah," said Joe. "I know… Hundreds of years ago a wolf escaped from some hunters by leaping off some rocks." As he spoke he glanced over Spiker's shoulder and noticed that there *was* a jagged rock face, just above the tree line.

"But don't forget the best bit. After it escaped," said Spiker, in a spooky voice, "the wolf came back and stalked the hunters, catching them one by one, ripping out their throats and crunching their bones..."

Matt grinned. "You made that bit up."

"And people say," added Spiker, his voice dropping to a ghoulish whisper, "that you can still hear the ghost of the wolf, howling in the woods at night..."

As he spoke, the wind picked up and a cloud drifted over the afternoon sun, darkening the sky. Joe shivered. After all the weird stuff he'd seen, thanks to Uncle Charlie's Egyptian amulet, he could just imagine a ghost wolf lurking in the forest watching and waiting...

"Hey, you lot!" came a shout. "If you've finished setting up your tent, I need some volunteers to help collect firewood!"

It was Lizzy – one of the campsite activity leaders. She was small and wiry, with short red hair. According to their teacher Miss Bruce, she was a champion rock climber. "Come on! It'll be dark before we get the fire built!"

By the time they had built the fire, the camp helpers had prepared a campfire dinner.

"I'm starving," said Joe, sitting down next to Matt, with a plate piled high with bangers and beans. There were twenty children from Joe's class there, along with Miss Bruce and the headmaster, Mr Hill. They sat together on logs arranged in a circle round the fire, tucking into their dinner.

As Joe shovelled in his last spoonful of beans he heard a strange noise in the distance...

AWWWHOOOOOOOOOOOO...

"What was that?"

Matt took a bite of sausage and shrugged. "I didn't hear anything."

AWWWHOOOOOOOOOO...

"Listen! There it is again!" Joe peered out, but it was getting dark and he couldn't see anything. "It's coming from over there."

Matt stopped scoffing for a second, and listened. Then he smiled impishly. "You're hearing things, Joe! Must be all the talk of ghosts freaking you out."

But before Joe could reply, Mr Hill blew a whistle to get everyone's attention. "When everyone's finished eating, I want you all to help tidy up. You lads over there," he said, pointing to Joe, Matt and a few others,

"collect the plates. And that group over there, you'll be on dishes tonight…" There were groans from the dishwashing group, but Mr Hill went on. "You'll be swapping jobs tomorrow night! Remember, camping is about teamwork – and everyone has to help. I remember when my wife and I went camping with friends in the Cairngorm Mountains. Everyone had to pitch in – especially when the blizzard started…"

Joe and Matt grinned at each other and rolled their eyes. Mr Hill had already spent the entire coach ride boring the class silly with stories about his camping adventures, and now he was off on another one. They quickly stacked the plates and carried them to the sinks.

"Want to hear a ghost story?" Ben said, putting his torch beam under his chin so that his face lit up like a ghoul. "It was a dark, stormy night, and a group of kids were camping in a creepy forest…"

AWWWHOOOOOOOOOO...

"Hey," Joe interrupted. "Did you hear that?"

"Not again!" giggled Matt. "What is it this time, Joe, not another ghostie?"

"No, it sounds like an animal howling."

"A ghost wolf?" said Matt. "Yeah, yeah, very funny, Joe!"

"Let's go take a look in the forest!" said Joe. "Come on."

"What? Now?" Ben glanced at the trees. "In the dark?"

Joe nodded. "Why not!"

"I'm in!" grinned Matt. "What about you, Ben?"

"Definitely!"

Joe pulled his torch out of his pocket. "Head for the tents," he whispered. "Everyone will think we've gone to fetch something. Then we can double back to the trees."

As they walked into the forest, the darkness

closed in. There was a distant rumble of thunder.

"This way," whispered Joe, heading for a path he'd spotted earlier. He flashed his torch left and right, the beam catching movements in the bushes. "Did you see that rat?"

"Yeah, it was massive," breathed Matt.

As they went deeper into the woods, the trees grew denser and the undergrowth thicker. There was no light from the moon now. Joe's heart beat faster. This was how Uncle Charlie must feel when he set off on an expedition!

There was another rumble of thunder, closer this time. And Joe heard the howling again, followed by the sound of twigs breaking and bushes being pushed aside. Something crashed through the bracken.

"I think it's over there!" Joe hissed, flashing his beam at the bushes. "Spread out."

Matt moved off left, Ben headed right, their torch beams bouncing around the trees. After a few minutes, Matt called back, "Do you see anything?"

"No!" Ben shouted.

Their voices were much further away than Joe expected. He was just about to call them when there was a sudden crack of lightning, and he saw a shape lunging towards him, its sharp teeth flashing white. It crashed into him, sending him flying.

He gasped, waiting for the wolf to lock him in its jaws and sink its fangs into him...

CHAPTER TWO

Joe felt a scratchy tongue lick his face. He opened his eyes – it was a big hairy dog!

"Hello, Joe," growled the dog. "I need your help!"

Joe gasped. The creature wasn't a ghost wolf – but it wasn't much better either. *Not another undead pet*, Joe thought. They wouldn't leave him alone!

Joe wriggled free, wiping sticky drool off his face with his sleeve. He flashed his torch in the animal's face. It wasn't a pretty sight. Green drool hung from its chops and its red eyes bulged out like snooker balls.

"Look, I'd like to help you, really I would," Joe shuffled uncomfortably, "but I'm on a school trip. I'm off duty as Protector of Undead Pets, OK!"

But it wasn't OK. The dog gave a deep throaty growl. Then its tail drooped. Its eyes boggled. And it started howling again.

"Stop it!" Joe hushed. He was pretty sure no one else could hear it. But the noise was horrendous!

AWWWHOOOOOOOOOOOO...

As the dog howled, its fur stood up on end.

"Look!" said Joe. "I can't help you. Clear off into the woods and stop making that noise!"

The dog did stop howling. But it wasn't listening to Joe any more. It was staring at something over his shoulder. Then its ears picked up and its tail began to wag. And…

"Squirrel!" it suddenly yelped. And it took off like a bullet.

For a few seconds Joe just stood there, wondering if the dog would come back. It didn't.

"Joe…? JOE!" Matt suddenly appeared by his side. "Are you OK? I thought I heard you shout."

"Yeah," said Ben, arriving a few seconds later. "You sounded like you were talking to someone."

"Er… I just tripped over a tree root," mumbled Joe.

Matt grinned. "And what about the noise you heard? Did you see anything?"

"Nope." Then Joe felt a few drops of rain on his head. "Maybe we should head back to camp. It's starting to rain…"

As they retraced their steps, they saw two

shadowy figures waiting for them. An enormous flashlight shone in their faces, making them blink. It was Mr Hill and Lizzy.

"Where have you been?" demanded Mr Hill.

Joe took a deep breath. "Er… We heard a noise and thought we'd take a look."

Lizzy smiled kindly. "Well, you're not the first, and you won't be the last. But it's camp rules – you're not allowed to head off on your own, OK?"

They nodded, studying their shoes intently.

"Go on then," said Mr Hill sternly. "Back to camp! And don't let me catch you wandering off by yourselves again, or you'll be on the first bus home!"

When they got back to their tent, Spiker was smirking. Joe's eyes narrowed. "Did you tell Mr Hill that we'd gone to the woods?"

Matt nudged him. "Better drop it, Joe. We don't want to get in more trouble tonight."

Joe scowled and rummaged around for his wash bag. They all got ready for bed in silence.

When Joe opened his eyes the next morning, the sun was shining. He wriggled out of his sleeping bag and pulled on his jeans. Just then a bell rang…

"Breakfast in ten minutes," Miss Bruce called. "Mr Hill's doing a fry-up!"

UNDEAD PETS

Spiker groaned. Ben buried his head in his sleeping bag. Matt looked groggy. Joe grabbed his toothbrush and headed for the washrooms.

But as he passed Mr Hill's tent, he heard a strange chomping noise. Joe froze. *No! No!* He groaned. *Please don't let it be that dog…*

Joe glanced across the camp. He could see Mr Hill busy cooking breakfast on the barbecue. He looked around to check no one was watching and stepped inside the headmaster's tent. He gasped. It was chaos. Clothes were strewn across the floor and right in the middle was the zombie dog, chomping through a packet of biscuits.

"What are you doing in here?" Joe said, grabbing the biscuits out of its mouth.

"Brian won't mind!" said the dog.

"Brian? Brian who?" Joe felt a lurch in his belly. "You don't mean Brian Hill? My headmaster?"

A stringy piece of green drool dribbled from the dog's mouth to the floor. "Yeah," it growled.

UNDEAD PETS

"My name's Dexter. I was Brian's dog."

Could this crazy animal really once have been his headmaster's pet?

"JOE EDMUNDS! WHAT IS THE MEANING OF THIS?"

Joe spun round. Mr Hill stood in the doorway, his face pulsating with rage.

Dexter started barking with excitement at the sight of his owner. But Mr Hill couldn't see or hear a thing.

He snatched the biscuits from Joe's hands. "How dare you go into someone else's tent and

touch their things? What on earth are you doing in here?"

A few weeks ago Joe had taken the blame when a zombie hamster had devoured Mr Hill's lunchbox. And now it looked like he'd have to do the same again.

"Er... Well..." Joe stammered, desperately trying to think of an excuse.

Mr Hill shook his head. "I'm not interested in hearing any of your feeble excuses. As punishment, you can wash the breakfast dishes! Now help me tidy up this mess."

CHAPTER THREE

As soon as Mr Hill let him go, Joe marched off to a quiet corner of the camp. He checked no one was around, then turned on Dexter. "You're nothing but trouble!"

"It's not my fault!" growled the dog. "You should help me!"

"I can't!" Joe sighed. "Now clear off! People will think I'm nuts if they see me talking to myself." He glanced over to the table where the class were lining up to collect their breakfast. He saw Spiker smirking over at him.

"And what's *he* looking at!" said Joe, scowling back.

"Who? Snot Shot?" said Dexter.

"What?"

"Snot Shot."

"What are you talking about?"

"That's what Brian calls him – he's got names for all of you! Silly names he uses when he's not at school."

Joe's brain boggled. "Funny nicknames? I didn't know Mr Hill had a sense of humour." Then he glanced over at Spiker again. "So why does he call him Snot Shot?"

But Dexter didn't need to explain, because right at that moment Spiker stuck his finger up his nose and had a good poke around, before taking out a bogey and flicking it at the kid in front of him.

"Come and have your breakfast," Miss Bruce yelled, spotting Joe hanging back from the group. "Before it's all gone."

"Before Hoover Head eats it!" added Dexter.

"Who's that?"

"Hoover Head – him, over there. That's what Brian calls him."

Joe glanced over to see Nick the Stick – the tallest lad in the class, piling his plate high with food.

"Come on, Joe!" called Miss Bruce again.

"Look, I've got to go," hissed Joe to Dexter.

He went to join the others and didn't look back.

"Hey, Joe, want a biscuit?" called Leonie, one of the girls in his class.

"No, he's already had some," sniggered Harry, Spiker's best mate.

There were a few giggles as Joe got his breakfast and went to sit down next to Matt.

"What's going on?" Joe whispered.

"Spiker heard Mr Hill telling you off for taking his biscuits," Matt replied. "And he's told everyone about it."

Joe looked around for Spiker, but he was nowhere to be seen. Dexter had disappeared too. He just hoped it was for good this time!

"Right!" called Lizzy. "Gather round and I'll tell you what we've got planned for today!"

Joe cheered up. This was more like it!

"In a few minutes we'll be starting the aerial adventure. The first part involves tackling the giant climbing wall, followed by a treetops wire walk…"

"YES!" Joe breathed.

"…When you reach the end, there's an amazing zip wire over the woods!"

The kids whispered to each other excitedly.

"Wait a minute," said Lizzy. "There's more! After lunch you'll be going underground into our tunnel trail for a treasure hunt. And finally, my favourite bit." She beamed as she spoke. "Tonight, we'll be taking you on a moonlight safari through the woods to see what wildlife you can spot."

"Like wolves?" Spiker shouted.

"Awhooooooooo!" howled Harry.

"Who knows," said Lizzy. "But before you go looking, you've got to get yourselves up that wall, so come on, follow me!"

"I'll never get up there!" wailed Leonie, as soon as she saw the climbing wall.

It was thirteen metres tall, with several routes up the side, colour-coded for difficulty. Two more instructors, Finn and James, were waiting for them at the wall, and a third, Chrissie, was already at the top.

"I'll climb first," said Lizzy, after showing

them how to put on the safety harness. "Then
you can follow, one at a time."

Lizzy was an amazing climber. Joe watched
her stay close against the wall, her hands and
feet easily finding the holds. She reached the
top in minutes.

"I definitely can't do that!" wailed Leonie. "It's too high!"

Joe was just about to tell her to put a sock in it when he spotted something even more annoying. Bounding through the trees towards him was Dexter.

"Who's next?" Lizzy called down.

Spiker shoved Joe forward. "Go on, superman!" he said sarcastically.

Joe was glad to go first so he could get away before Dexter started bothering him again! But the dog was too fast. He arrived just as Joe was stepping into the harness.

"Are you ready to help me now?" barked the dog, leaping about at Joe's feet and letting off an enormous fart.

Joe ignored Dexter, but it was impossible to ignore the stink that surrounded him.

"Urghhh!" groaned Spiker, holding his nose. "What's *that*?" Then he sniggered. "Have you pooed your pants, Joe? Is the climb too scary for you?"

"Shut up, Spiker!" said Joe, but some of the other kids were already giggling.

"Settle down," said Mr Hill sternly. "Come on, Joe! Get going!"

Joe found the handholds easily and in just a few minutes, he was halfway up. Another five minutes and he was pulling himself over the top.

Lizzy beamed at him. "You're a natural!"

But before Joe could say anything, he heard a howl from the bottom of the wall. He could see Dexter scrabbling about, as though he was trying to climb up after him, before finally giving up and bounding away.

UNDEAD PETS

Ben and Matt were next up the wall, followed by Abby and then Leonie, who was making such a fuss that James had to climb next to her.

Spiker followed soon after, and once a few more joined them, Lizzy and Finn led them on to the treetops challenge.

"The wire walk is thirty metres long and zig-zags through the treetops," said Finn. "There are ropes to hold on to and a rope to walk along. Ready?"

Joe nodded, but Ben didn't look keen.

"It's perfectly safe," said Finn. "The harness will stop you from falling. I'll go first."

"Don't look down!" Ben said, as he, Matt and Joe began inching their way along.

Joe didn't mind heights. He followed the wire, weaving in and out of the tall pines. But then he spotted Dexter again, racing backwards and forwards down on the ground and barking up at him. "Help me, Joe! Help me!"

UNDEAD PETS

Joe tried to ignore him.

"Ready for the zip wire?" Finn called, as Joe reached the final platform. "You go first, and Chrissie will be waiting for you at the end, OK?"

Joe nodded, giving his harness a final tug to make sure it was secure.

"Go, Joe!" Matt yelled, as Joe took off, whizzing down the wire.

UNDEAD PETS

"Wow!" Joe breathed. The trees whistled past and the ground was a blur – he felt like a character in an action film ... until his harness jerked him to a stop at the bottom and he waggled about in midair, like a fish on a hook.

Chrissie caught him and helped him down. Joe's legs felt like jelly, but he was buzzing from the ride. Then he felt his excitement fall apart like a soggy tissue! Dexter was waiting.

The dog launched himself at Joe, crashing into him and smothering his face in drool.

"Hey! Cut it out!" grimaced Joe.

Dexter's breath smelled like a sweaty armpit.

"But you don't understand!" growled the dog. "I can't pass over until you help me.

I'm fed up with waiting!"

Joe sighed. It had always been his dream to have a dog and he would have loved one like Dexter – if he had been alive. "OK, OK," Joe said. "Tell me what you need me to do."

"Really? You'll help me now?"

"I'll try. But hurry!" Joe glanced up at the top of the zip wire. "As soon as the others get down, I won't be able to talk to you." He could see Leonie having her harness attached.

Dexter glanced up too. "Oh dear, Moanie Leonie is coming."

Joe grinned. Moanie Leonie must be another one of Mr Hill's nicknames – it suited her. "Come on then, tell me what happened."

But now he had Joe's attention, Dexter didn't seem to know what to do with himself. He scratched his ears and chewed his tail, then jumped up and down and started pacing around. Finally it came tumbling out…

Brian loved taking me on long walks...

But the trouble was, I wasn't good at doing what he told me.

Sometimes I'd get lost.

Brian tried to train me. But it was so boring! I just liked to do my own thing.

Then one day I chased a squirrel...

And I ran right off a cliff.

"The trouble is, Brian blames himself for the accident," Dexter went on.

"Why?"

"Because he couldn't train me. He tried his best. But I'm not that sort of a dog. I like to be free. Run wild…"

Dexter suddenly turned his head, and began staring at something in the trees. His ears pricked up. His tail began to wag, and then…

"Rabbit!" he yelped. He was about to run after it, when Joe made a dive for him.

"Hold up!" said Joe. "You haven't told me what you want me to do yet."

"What?" Dexter was straining to get free, his boggle eyes darting left and right, searching for the rabbit he'd spied.

"What do you need *me* for?" said Joe.

"To make Brian see that it wasn't his fault I died."

"What? Mr Hill isn't going to listen to me!"

But Dexter wasn't interested any more. The smell of the rabbit was too much. He jerked free of Joe's arms, and shot off into the trees like a bullet.

CHAPTER FOUR

"I hate egg mayonnaise!" groaned Ava, as she unwrapped her roll. "I wanted ham!"

"And I hate cheese!" added Bethany, who was peering at her lunch as though it was a specimen in a jar.

They were all back at the camp now, eating lunch round the log circle before the treasure hunt. Joe could see Dexter chasing around the other side of the camp, chewing twigs and sniffing out squirrels.

As he got up to put his rubbish in the bin,

Undead Pets

Joe could hear Mr Hill chatting to Lizzy. "My dog, Dexter, would have loved it here. There's so much space to run around…" He sighed. "Mind you, I'd have spent all day trying to get him back on his lead afterwards."

"Mr Hill! I've lost my water bottle…" wailed Leonie. "I think I left it in the woods!"

Moanie Leonie, Joe thought. Maybe Mr Hill was funnier than he looked!

Just then Dexter came hurtling out of the trees and shook himself – splattering Joe with mud. "So *when* are you going to speak to Brian?"

Joe made a face. "I don't know. I haven't worked out what to say to him!"

The dog sat down at Joe's feet and gave a long melancholy howl.

"Don't start that again!" muttered Joe.

But Dexter continued howling. Joe stuck his fingers in his ears and looked over his shoulder to check no one was watching him. "Look," he said. "I'd really like to help you. But I can't just go and tell Mr Hill it's not his fault you died! How do you think I'm going to explain that I know about you falling off that cliff?"

Dexter kept howling. Louder and louder…

"If only there was some way of showing Mr Hill that it's not his fault. If he could see that not all dogs are like you, Dexter — that some dogs *do* respond to commands and do what they're told, instead of just taking off whenever they want," Joe said.

Dexter stopped howling and cocked his head to one side.

"*Then* perhaps he'd realize that it wasn't his fault you got yourself killed. After all, he tried everything to keep you safe, didn't he?"

Just then Lizzy called, "Tunnel treasure-hunt time! Follow me!"

Joe stood up. "Look, I've got to go. But I'll try to think of something, OK?"

But Dexter wasn't listening any more. He'd spotted something more interesting in the trees. He took off like a rocket.

"Everyone gather round," called Lizzy.

They were on the other side of the camp now, near the start of the tunnel trail. Joe peered over at the tunnels. There were five of them, dug into the side of a grassy bank.

"It's a bit like an underground maze," said Lizzy. "You'll need to crawl down each tunnel and look for the nine letters of the alphabet that we've hidden inside. Write the letters on your sheets, and when you've found all of them, rearrange the letters into a word."

"I love anagrams!" breathed Abby.

Joe nudged Matt. "What's an anagram?"

"Sounds like some sort of anorak," he grinned. "A brown one your nan would wear!"

UNDEAD PETS

"Listen now!" said Lizzy. "When you've solved the word puzzle, use the map we've given you to come and find me in the forest. The first pair to reach me with the correct word is the winner."

"Want to team up?" asked Matt.

Joe nodded. "Definitely!"

Everyone else was getting into pairs, too. Ben and Thomas. The twins Ava and Molly. And Spiker and Harry, who weren't normally allowed to work together because they messed about so much. Miss Bruce didn't seem to have noticed today.

"Not sure I'll fit in there," said Nick the Stick, bending down to peer into one of the tunnels.

"Well, I can, so you can, too!" grinned Finn, puffing out his chest so he looked even more enormous. "But if you get stuck, I'll haul you out, OK?"

"Don't forget your waterproofs," said Lizzy. "It's damp and muddy in there. And you'll need helmets, too!"

"What if we bump into each other?" said Bethany.

"Only two pairs are allowed in each tunnel at a time," said Finn. "And all the tunnels lead through to the other side of the bank, so you don't need to come back the way you go in."

"Everyone ready?" called Lizzy. "Then get going!"

Joe and Matt raced for the largest tunnel, beating Spiker and Harry, but only just.

"Watch it!" growled Matt, as Spiker and

UNDEAD PETS

Harry tried to push them out of the way.

"Watch it yourself," smirked Harry.

"Give them a minute to get inside," said Finn, holding Spiker and Harry back. "Then you can follow. But keep your distance."

The tunnel was about a metre wide and it had a damp, musty smell. They crawled through, ducking their heads under the low ceiling of the tunnel. After they'd gone a few metres inside, the only light was from their torches and it was hard to tell where they were going or where they'd

UNDEAD PETS

been. There were a few dead ends and false turns.

"Hey!" shouted Matt, as Spiker and Harry barged past them. But Joe didn't really care. He was thinking about Uncle Charlie's adventure at an underground pyramid. Joe could imagine how Uncle Charlie must have felt, inching his way through the gloom. He shone his torch ahead, half expecting to find a pile of bones!

"Got it!" Joe shouted, as he spotted the first letter, fixed to the side of the tunnel. It was a W!

More letters followed soon after...

"Come on," Joe called to Matt, as he crawled into another tunnel. "We've only got two more to find! Wait – what was that scratching noise?"

Matt grinned. "Rats?"

"Hope not!" Joe grimaced.

But just then something big and wet loomed out of the darkness. And it definitely wasn't a rat.

"Urgghh," Joe groaned, as Dexter licked his face, smothering him in sticky ghoul drool. "Cut it out! I'm not an ice cream!"

"I've found something," Dexter panted. "In the forest! Come and see!"

"What was that about ice cream?" called Matt, who was a bit further back.

"Er, nothing!" Joe turned to Dexter and silently mouthed, "WAIT OUTSIDE!"

Dexter shot back down the tunnel, his muddy tail splattering Joe in the face.

UNDEAD PETS

Five minutes later, the boys scrambled out of the exit, blinking in the daylight.

"Come on!" shouted Matt, "We can rearrange the letters on the way!" He broke into a run, heading for the trees.

Joe looked around for Dexter, just as the dog crashed out of the bushes and hurtled past them. Luckily he seemed to be heading the same way.

"Hey, Joe!" barked Dexter. "Guess what I found in the woods!"

Joe shrugged. It was impossible to talk with Matt just a few metres in front of them.

"A well-behaved dog!" woofed Dexter. "Just like you said – one that does what it's told! You've got to see it. This way!" He veered left.

Joe slowed to a jog, then to a walk. Dexter wanted them to go a different way to where the map was taking them.

"Come on! It's not far!" Dexter barked impatiently.

UNDEAD PETS

Joe hesitated for a second, then he stuffed the map in his pocket. "Er, I think it's down here, Matt," he said, heading left.

"Are you sure?"

"Definitely! Come on…"

It was a narrow path, with several sawn-off tree stumps along the way. The ground was much more overgrown than the trail they'd been following before.

After a few minutes, Matt stopped. "Are you sure this is the right way? I haven't seen anyone else. Maybe we should check the map again…"

As Joe handed the map over to Matt he could hear the sound of barking close by. And this time it wasn't Dexter.

CHAPTER FIVE

Joe peered through the trees. A little further down the path he could see a small cottage. In the garden a couple of kids were playing with some puppies. Dexter was with them, leaping around and chasing his tail!

"We've definitely taken the wrong path," said Matt, still looking at the map. "We should have turned right back there…"

But Joe wasn't listening. He took a few steps closer to the garden. And as he did, a twig snapped under his foot. The children looked over. There was a boy about his age and a younger girl who looked about six.

"Are you lost?" shouted the boy. He had a freckly face with reddish hair. As he spoke, the puppies started barking loudly. "Quiet!" he said firmly and they settled down straight away.

"See!" barked Dexter. "They do as they're told. We need to show Brian!"

"Are you looking for the campsite?" the boy asked.

Before Joe could reply, Matt spoke up. "No, we're not, thanks!" He turned to Joe. "Come on, we need to get back now."

"Are they all your dogs?" Joe asked.

"Yeah, they're still puppies, really. Come and have a look, if you want."

Matt rolled his eyes. "What about the treasure hunt?"

Joe ignored him and went into the garden. Matt would hate him for spoiling the treasure hunt, but he'd have to worry about that later.

Strangely, the puppies didn't come running to him, even though their bottoms were wriggling, and their tails were wagging. They were lovely looking dogs with droopy ears and thick coats.

"You've got them really well trained," Joe said.

The boy nodded. "They're an easy breed to train. My dad works in the forest, and there's so much to distract the dogs that they have to be easy to control!" Then he nodded to the pups and they zoomed over to Joe, their short stumpy tails wagging like crazy.

Dexter began barking excitedly. "Take one back to Brian!"

Joe made a face. It wasn't as if he could just put one in his pocket! "Are they spaniels?"

The boy nodded. "Yeah... I wish we could keep them all. But Dad says we need to find homes for them soon."

Dexter started howling with excitement. "Let's get one for Brian!"

Joe paused for a moment. If Mr Hill got a new dog – a better-behaved one – then all his guilt about Dexter might disappear. But Joe had no idea how to persuade Mr Hill that he wanted another dog.

"My name's Tom," said the boy. "And this is my sister, Rachel. Are you camping at Wolf's Leap?"

"Yeah, we're staying until tomorrow. I'm Joe – and this is Matt."

Matt smiled briefly, then glanced at his watch. "Come on, Joe. We're running out of time."

"We've got to go," said Joe reluctantly. "Thanks for letting us see the puppies."

As he and Matt walked back down the forest path, Joe was thinking hard. Somehow they had to get Mr Hill to meet the pups. But how?

"What's the plan?" barked Dexter, chasing around Joe's feet. "What are you going to do?"

Joe shrugged. It was impossible to talk with Matt close by.

Just then they heard Lizzy's whistle.

Matt groaned. "Someone's finished the treasure hunt."

"And I bet I know who," muttered Joe.

A few moments later Joe's fears were realized. He nudged Matt, "Look over there."

Through the trees, they could see Leonie and Abby walking proudly back to camp with Lizzy in between them.

"What kept you, Joe?" called Leonie as she passed by.

Joe made a face.

"If only we hadn't taken that wrong turn," sighed Matt. "Then we'd have beaten them easily."

"Yeah, sorry about that," muttered Joe, scuffing the ground with his shoe. "I'm not sure how I managed to muddle up the map. "

"What were you thinking?" Matt suddenly sounded exasperated. "It was so easy to follow…"

"Er… Well, I just got distracted…"

"Yeah," said Matt gloomily. "You seem to get distracted a lot lately. And it's usually when there are animals around! If you hadn't stopped to pet those dogs we might still have won."

Joe's face reddened. Matt was right. The undead pets were taking over his life!

Just then Dexter crashed out of the bushes. "Have you got a plan yet?"

Joe glared at him. "No!" he muttered, hoping

UNDEAD PETS

Matt wouldn't hear. Then silently he mouthed: "GO AWAY!" He turned back to Matt, but his mate was already stalking off back to camp, his head down, his hands stuffed into his pockets. He looked miserable. Joe sighed. He hated falling out with Matt. He raced after him, but as they reached camp, Leonie and Abby were already collecting their prizes – a pair of cool-looking head torches.

"Well done, girls," beamed Lizzy. "You weren't the first ones to find me, but you were the only ones who'd worked out the word puzzle. And just in case anyone is still struggling, the word was 'Wolfhound'!"

Matt slapped his forehead. "Of course!"

But Joe wasn't listening. He'd heard a howl…

AWWWHOOOOOOOOOO…

Dexter was at it again — trying to get his attention. Joe could see him in the distance, skulking around the trees just beyond the camp, howling his head off! Joe sighed. Somehow he had to get Mr Hill to see those dogs. But he had no idea how to do it.

CHAPTER SIX

"Has everyone got their torch?"

It was dark now and the class were getting ready for the night walk. Dexter was sitting next to Joe, fidgeting and scratching. Every so often, he'd stop to ask if Joe had thought of a plan yet.

"No!" he muttered. "Stop asking!"

Lizzy called for quiet. "I'm going to split you into two teams. Mr Hill and I will take one group," she said. "And the other group will go with Miss Bruce and James. Let's see whose team can spot the most wildlife tonight!"

Leonie nudged Abby as Lizzy divided them into two teams. "We'll spot loads with our new torches!" They started dazzling each other with the beams.

"Remember," said Mr Hill sternly. "Stick together and don't go wandering off on your own. I don't want to spend the rest of the night looking for you!"

Joe froze. And then an idea erupted in his brain. Suppose he got himself lost, near Tom's cottage. Then Mr Hill would have to come and find him. And if he did, then maybe he'd meet the pups!

Joe looked over at the dark forest. Could he really find his way to the cottage in the dark, all by himself? Maybe not – but surely Dexter could.

"All ready?" asked Lizzy.

Joe put up his hand. "I need the toilet!"

Everyone groaned. Mr Hill shook his head despairingly.

"I'm really desperate," pleaded Joe. He had to tell Dexter his plan. And the toilets were the only place where no one else would hear.

"Go on then," sighed Mr Hill. "But make it quick!"

As he turned to go, Joe beckoned to Dexter to follow him.

"So, are you sure you'll be able to find the cottage again?"

"Mmm?" Dexter was concentrating on scratching his ear.

"Have you listened to anything I've been telling you?" Joe puffed out his cheeks. "I've explained this three times, and you still don't look like you've heard a word."

"Of course I have!" growled Dexter.

"And you're sure you'll find your way?"

"I'm part bloodhound! Bloodhounds can smell really well."

Joe looked sceptical. Wasn't this the dog that always got lost when he went out with Mr Hill?

But it was too late to worry. Joe could hear Lizzy calling him. He hurried back to his group and they set off.

"Remember to be quiet and keep your eyes open," she said as she led them down the path into the woods.

The night air felt cold on their faces and their torch beams bounced off trees and bushes.

"Will we see any badgers?" whispered Simon.

"Maybe," Lizzy whispered. "But we'll have to be extra quiet to stand a chance. Keep a look out for bats and foxes, too."

UNDEAD PETS

"And ghost wolves!" cackled Spiker, as he and Harry pushed past to get nearer the front.

Joe tried to stay at the back, but Mr Hill had the same idea. He was making sure no one got left behind.

"Don't you go wandering off again!" he whispered to Joe and Matt. "And stop dawdling!"

UNDEAD PETS

"Sorry, Mr Hill," Joe mumbled. "I just don't want to miss anything." He flashed his beam into the undergrowth, but the headmaster didn't look convinced. Joe sighed. Getting lost was going to be difficult.

Dexter was scampering along by Joe's side, but suddenly he veered off the path, disappearing into a clump of ferns.

"Hurry up, you two!" snapped Mr Hill, shooing him along again. "You don't want to get left behind!"

Yes I do, thought Joe glumly. At this rate he was never going to get away!

But just then there was a ruckus further down the line.

"Hey!" hissed Mr Hill. "What's going on?" He moved forward.

Suddenly something cold and damp brushed the back of Joe's hand. It was Dexter.

"That way," he growled, nodding to the left. "That's the way to the cottage."

Joe flashed his torch. He didn't recognize anything. He definitely couldn't see the path with the tree stumps that he'd been on earlier. "Are you sure?" he whispered.

But Dexter was already heading off.

Joe was about to follow, when he saw Mr Hill coming back down the line. "Pants!" he muttered.

Just then there was a whisper from the front of the line. "Badgers up ahead, everyone turn off their torches and be quiet!"

As the beams went out, Joe inched away from the group. He nudged Matt. "I think I saw a fox. I'm going to take a look."

"But you'll miss the badgers!"

UNDEAD PETS

"Back in a minute…" And then he crept away.

"Joe!" Matt called.

"Quiet!" Mr Hill hissed.

And Joe was free. He moved quietly through the bracken following Dexter. But the dog was going much too fast – bounding ahead, leaping over ferns and fallen branches, leaving Joe behind.

"Wait for me!" Joe whispered. He shone his torch around a bit, but he didn't recognize anything from the afternoon. "Are you sure this is the right way?"

"Yes," barked Dexter. "Come on!" He bounded off into the forest ahead of Joe.

"Dexter?" Joe searched the trees with his torch. "Dexter? Where are you?" He listened. But all he could hear was the sound of the wind rustling the leaves above him. Joe shivered. Suddenly the dark woods felt slightly spooky. He was entirely on his own. He was also totally and utterly lost!

CHAPTER SEVEN

"Dexter? Where are you?"

Joe shone his beam to the left and right. But there was nothing but tall ferns, knee-high grasses and a wall of giant trees looming menacingly over him. A dark shadow flitted past. Something else moved in the bushes to his right. Up above there was a fluttering of wings. The creatures of the forest were everywhere. Joe's heart beat faster. Then suddenly he heard a howling in the distance.

AWWWHOOOOOOOOOO...

"Dexter?" Joe whispered. He began to move slowly towards the sound, carefully edging around uprooted tree stumps and sunken burrows.

AWWWHOOOOOOOOOOO...

The wind was stronger now, and the trees swayed and moaned, their branches creaking and groaning. Bats fluttered above. Owls watched from the trees and tiny scratchy rodents scurried over his feet.

AWWWHOOOOOOOOOOO...

"I'm coming, Dexter!" Joe called. His torch picked out a few old sawn-off tree stumps. Then the ground became flatter, and he spotted a path, snaking off to the right. And suddenly the surroundings looked familiar. He'd done it! There was a crashing of branches, and Dexter hurtled towards him.

"There you are! I thought I'd lost you!"

Joe frowned. "What are you talking about? Your howling guided me here."

Dexter cocked his head to one side. "I wasn't howling."

"*What?*"

If it wasn't Dexter, what was it? Joe glanced around the dark trees, their branches creaking eerily in the wind. A cold shiver crackled down his spine. "Come on. Let's get to the cottage."

Once they were on the proper path it was easy to find the cottage. Joe wasn't looking forward to this bit – telling lies about being lost. As he knocked on the door, the puppies started barking inside. A man's voice hushed them and the door opened.

The forester was big and bearded. He towered over Joe. But then his face crumpled

into a smile and Joe breathed a sigh of relief.
"Hello, there," he said. "What can I do for you?"

"Er, hello, my name is Joe Edmunds. I was on
a night safari from the camp and I got lost…"

"You'd better come in," said Tom's dad. "I'm
Paul Frost. Were you with Lizzy French?"

Joe nodded.

"I'll dig out her number and tell her you're
OK. You're not the first kid who's turned up on
our doorstep!"

UNDEAD PETS

Dexter headed straight for the living room where the pups were barking and whining and scratching at the door.

"I'll try calling Lizzy now. The signal's not always great in the forest," Paul warned. "But if we can't reach her, we can always walk you back to the campsite."

That was the last thing Joe wanted! If Mr Hill didn't come to the cottage, the plan would be a washout!

There was an agonizing silence and then...

"Hello, Lizzy? It's Paul Frost here – yeah, from Foxglove Cottage. One of the boys from the camp has appeared on my doorstep!"

Joe shifted his feet. He could just imagine the look on Mr Hill's face.

"Yes, Joe Edmunds, that's right." There was a pause and then, "Oh yes, fine. See you soon."

The plan was working so far, but Joe was in for a major telling-off. He'd probably be in detention until he was twelve!

Paul put the phone down and smiled at Joe. "They're on their way. Do you like dogs? My children are playing with some spaniel puppies in here. I'll just go and put the kettle on."

Joe opened the door to the living room. The puppies were racing around, jumping over Rachel and Tom, chewing each other's tails and barking like mad.

"Hi," said Tom. "Did you get lost again?"

"Yeah," Joe said awkwardly. "I recognized the path and so I was able to find your house…" He was terrible at making stuff up. He stroked one of the puppies and tried to think of something else to say.

UNDEAD PETS

Dexter couldn't sit still. He kept jumping up at the window then dashing through to the kitchen, listening out for Mr Hill. "What if he won't come in!" he barked, as he made another return journey to the living room. "He needs to meet the pups properly."

Joe ignored him. There was nothing he could do but wait.

CHAPTER EIGHT

There was a loud knock on the door. All the kids from his group were there. Moanie Leonie and Abby, Ava and Molly, Simon, Ben, Spiker, Harry and Matt, plus Lizzy and Mr Hill. It had started to rain and they all looked fed up — except Mr Hill, who looked furious. His face was purple and he was glaring at Joe!

"Hi, Paul," said Lizzy. "Thanks for looking after Joe for us. This is Brian Hill, his headmaster."

"Hello," said Paul. "It's no problem at all. Would you like to come in for a drink?"

"No!" snapped Spiker. "We haven't found the ghost wolf yet!"

"Yeah," wailed Leonie. "The other team will have seen loads more stuff than us! I wanted *our* team to win the competition."

Mr Hill shot them a look for their rudeness. Then he turned to Paul. "It's kind of you, but we should be getting back to the camp."

Yeah, so he can give me a proper telling-off, thought Joe glumly. Somehow he had to get Mr Hill inside the house to see the pups...

But just then Dexter came to the rescue. He raced back into the house, and pushed open the living-room door. The puppies came bounding out, spilling on to the doorstep. The children gasped in delight and rushed forward to pet the pups as they whizzed around, wagging their tails.

"Aw, they're so cute," said Molly. "Look at their tiny tails!"

"Ha! That one seems to like your trainers, Spiker," laughed Matt, as the largest puppy made a grab for Spiker's shoelace and began chewing it.

"Hey!" yelled Spiker, trying to shake him off. "Cut it out!"

"Heel!" commanded Paul. The puppies returned to his side at once.

Mr Hill raised his eyebrows. "They're well trained."

"They have to be to live in a forest."

Mr Hill bent down to stroke one of the puppies. "Hello there."

Joe held his breath. But it wasn't going to happen. Mr Hill stood up and his face was stern again. "We need to get going."

"No!" yelped Dexter. "Make him stay, Joe!"

But before Joe could say anything there was a distant roll of thunder and suddenly it started pouring with rain.

"Quick! Come in!" Paul said, holding open the door.

A couple of the children made a dash for it and the others followed. Mr Hill reluctantly headed inside, too, still glowering at Joe.

"What are the pups called?" Ava asked, as everyone crowded into the kitchen.

"This one's Queenie," Rachel explained, scooping up the largest pup. "She's definitely the boss – she keeps the others in line. That one over there is Buttons – he's the clown. That's Munchie, the greedy one. And the small one is Titch."

"Do you want to give the puppies some treats?" asked Tom, handing a tin to Ava.

She bent down with the biscuits and the pups came hurtling towards her. But Titch wasn't with them. Joe spotted the little pup over by Mr Hill, who was tickling her ears while he talked to Paul.

Yes! thought Joe. *It's working!*

"I tried everything to train him," Mr Hill was saying. "But Dexter just didn't seem to be able to learn…"

"Well, it depends on the dog," replied Paul. "All breeds are different. Some of them are just naturally wilder than others. Even if you start training them as pups, some don't respond."

Joe glanced down at Dexter, who was scratching and fidgeting. He definitely wasn't the right sort of dog for Mr Hill.

"But I can't help thinking it was my fault," said the headmaster. "I don't think I was good at giving Dexter the right commands."

"Rubbish!" Paul smiled. "It was probably just his nature. Look, that pup's obviously taken a shine to you. Why don't you walk over to the other side of the room and call her to heel. Go on, see what happens."

Mr Hill didn't look keen. "No, er, I don't think so."

"Go on," called Molly. "Me and Ava have got a spaniel at home, and she's so clever!"

The headmaster frowned. Then he stood up and walked across the room to the door. "Heel!" he said, sounding slightly embarrassed. In a flash the pup trotted over to him and sat at his feet waiting for his next instruction.

A few of the kids clapped and Mr Hill's face turned pink.

"See!" laughed Paul. "I told you. Spaniels might be a bit noisy, but they're easy to train. We're actually trying to find homes for these puppies. You wouldn't be interested, would you?"

"Definitely not," said Mr Hill, his smile disappearing. "It's much too soon after Dexter."

"No, it's not!" yelped Dexter, leaping up and down. "Do something, Joe!"

But there was nothing he could do.

"I think it's time we went back to camp," Mr Hill said stiffly.

CHAPTER NINE

The kids trooped outside with Dexter trailing behind.

"We'll take the short cut," said Lizzy, leading the group on to a proper forest road. It was wide and open, and the moon lit the path.

Dexter immediately took off on his own. Joe was glad to see him go.

"I wish we'd seen more badgers," said Simon glumly.

"Yeah, we're bound to have lost the competition!" wailed Leonie. "The other group will have spotted heaps more!"

"And we've walked *so* much," Abby added.

"Yeah – all thanks to 'Where's Wally'!" added Spiker, poking Joe hard in the back.

Joe gave Spiker a filthy look and trudged on. He looked at Matt, who was walking next to him, but Matt was staring off into the distance and looking grumpy. He guessed his friend still hadn't forgiven him.

When they'd almost reached camp, Joe heard the howling again.

"What was that?" said Molly.

Ava linked her arm through her sister's. "Yeah, that's creepy…"

Joe gasped. "Can you lot hear it, too?"

Ben nodded. "Yes."

Joe gulped. So it wasn't Dexter howling!

"It's probably the ghost wolf," smirked Spiker. "Howling its head off before coming here to hunt us down and rip out our throats!"

Leonie gave a squeal and clutched Abby's arm tightly.

"In your dreams, Bradley," laughed Lizzy. "I've been working in these woods for three years, and I've never seen the ghost wolf yet!"

Matt nudged Joe. "I think it *was* the ghost wolf," he whispered. "And I bet the other group back at camp didn't hear it! A bunch of badgers and bats can't beat hearing a wolf!"

Joe smiled at his friend and gave a sigh of relief. It looked like he was forgiven!

Joe got his telling-off just before bed.

"How could you be so selfish?" the headmaster boomed. "Anything could have happened to you – and not only were you putting *yourself* in danger, but the rest of the group, too!"

Joe looked at his shoes.

"I've a good mind to call your parents!"

Joe winced. This was it. He was about to be sent home.

"I won't," added Mr Hill, his voice dropping. "But you're on your final warning, Joe Edmunds. And as punishment, you can wash the breakfast dishes again tomorrow morning!"

Was that it? Joe looked up at his headmaster. Surely Mr Hill was going to come up with something worse than greasy plates?

"Go on, now! Back to your tent!"

UNDEAD PETS

When Joe got back to the tent, Dexter was already there, spread out across the sleeping bags. It stank! Joe rolled his eyes. "The others will be here soon. Why don't you go and find somewhere else to sleep?"

"I can't sleep. Not until you sort out my problems," whined Dexter.

Joe gritted his teeth. He was tired and fed up and he'd had enough of Dexter for one night. "I tried my best. But I don't think Mr Hill is ready for a new pet, OK?"

Dexter gave a howl.

"And don't start that again!" Joe sighed. "Maybe Mr Hill doesn't need a new pet. After all, he's seen the pups now – so he knows not all dogs are as badly behaved as you, Dexter, and I'm sure he realizes that it wasn't his fault that you ran off a cliff! So, I was thinking … maybe it's time for you to go off now. You know, pass over to the other side…"

"No!" howled Dexter. "Brian needs a new dog!"

"But he doesn't want one!"

"He does!"

"Well, sort it out yourself, then," snapped Joe. "Because I've run out of ideas! Now budge up so I can get into my sleeping bag."

But Dexter wouldn't move. He sat there like a rock, glowering at Joe. "You must help me," he growled. "It's your job."

"Well, I wish it wasn't! I've had enough of being the Protector of Undead Pets… Now move over!" And he gave Dexter a shove.

AWWWHOOOOOOOOOOOOOOOOOOOOOOO…

UNDEAD PETS

"Stop that!" yelled Joe, shouting to be heard over Dexter howling.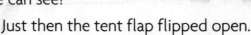
"I wish I could make another wish on the amulet. If I could, I would wish that I'd never seen it – and then maybe I wouldn't be stuck in the forest with a stinky zombie dog that no one else can see!"

Just then the tent flap flipped open.

"What was that about a zombie dog that no one else can see?"

Joe gulped. It was Matt.

"Who are you talking to, Joe?"

For a second he considered telling Matt the truth – the whole truth – about the amulet, the wish and all the weird undead pets that were haunting him. But there was no way Matt

93

would believe him. No one would! Joe sighed. "I was just … er … making up a ghost story."

But Matt didn't look like he believed him. "You've been acting really weird lately. And not just here… A few weeks ago you were obsessed with hamsters, then there was that freaky business with the alley cat. And now it's all about dogs! What's going on, Joe?"

"Er … well…"

Matt folded his arms. "Did you really get lost tonight, or did you do it on purpose?"

Joe felt his face turn red. "What! Of course I got lost."

Matt's eyes bored into him. "And what is the amulet?"

Joe froze. He wasn't sure what to say. He didn't want to lie to his best mate. But how could he tell him the truth?

Before he got a chance to say anything, Dexter farted and an invisible cloud of toxic zombie stink filled the tent.

"Gross!" Matt grimaced.

Joe pushed open the tent flap and pretended to waft the smell outside, but at the same time he gestured to Dexter to go.

"I'll be back!" growled the dog, as he darted out into the night.

Even with Dexter gone, the stink lingered.

"Urghh! What's that pong?" said Ben, as he and Spiker appeared moments later.

"That's foul!" Spiker clutched his throat as if he was about to throw up. "Was that you, Joe?"

"Yep, it was," Joe replied. "And if you don't shut up, I'll do another one in your face, Spiker!"

Matt sniggered. Ben grinned. And for once Spiker was speechless.

CHAPTER TEN

When Joe opened his eyes the next morning, the others were already heading for the washrooms.

"Want me to wait?" asked Matt.

"Nah, go ahead. I'll be there in a minute," Joe said. He was keen to avoid any more awkward questions!

Joe sighed. It was their last morning in camp, and he still hadn't solved Dexter's problems, which meant the dog would be coming home with him. He could almost hear his mum sneezing already! He pulled the sleeping bag up over his head and wished he'd never seen the amulet.

But just then there was a scrabbling noise and Dexter dived into the tent.

"Wake up, Joe!" he barked. "Something amazing has happened!"

As Joe poked his head out of his sleeping bag, a stringy dribble of green drool dropped out of the dog's mouth.

"Eurgh!" said Joe, closing his eyes.

"Get up!" said Dexter, pawing at the sleeping bag.

"Why, what's happened?"

"Last night I went into Brian's tent. But he didn't sleep much…"

Your zombie-dog breath probably kept him awake! thought Joe.

"Brian got up really early this morning, and went for a walk in the woods. So I followed him. Guess where he went?"

UNDEAD PETS

Joe shrugged.

"The cottage!"

"To see the puppies?"

"Yep!" barked Dexter. "And he's headed back to camp now with a puppy!"

"What?" Joe sat up. "Are you sure?"

"Come and see!"

Joe forgot he was still in his PJs, and followed Dexter outside, just in time to see Mr Hill walk into camp. And at his feet was Titch – the smallest of the puppies.

"Wow!" breathed Joe.

"Morning, Joe," called the headmaster as he passed Joe's tent. "As you can see, I've decided to get a new dog after all."

"That's great!"

"I suppose I've got you to thank, haven't I?" said Mr Hill. "If you hadn't wandered off by yourself last night, then I'd never have met Mr Frost." Mr Hill beamed at Joe.

"Does that mean I don't have to do the dishes?" Joe blurted out.

"Don't push your luck!" Mr Hill said, his usual expression returning.

Joe was in the camp kitchen, washing the last of the greasy plates when Dexter came to find him.

"I think it's time I went now," he said.

Joe wiped his soapy hands on his jeans. "Are you sure?"

"Yep, I feel ready now. This puppy is much better for Brian than I ever was. She's not a free spirit like me so they'll be happy together."

Joe looked at his feet. He never knew what to say when the undead pets passed over. Then he had a thought. "Er, Dexter, before you go, I was wondering… You know you told me about the nicknames Mr Hill has for some of the kids at school. Well, I was wondering what he calls *me*."

"Yogi!"

"What?"

"Yogi Bear!"

Joe frowned. "I look nothing like a bear!"

"Yogi Bear pinches picnic baskets and Brian said you pinched his lunch."

Joe's face turned pink. "It was an undead hamster that pinched it!" he said. "I just got the blame!" Still, there were worse nicknames.

"Goodbye, Joe," said Dexter. "Thanks for everything."

# UNDEAD PETS

Just as he started to fade, Dexter spotted something in the distance that Joe couldn't see, and with a shout of "SQUIRREL!" he vanished completely.

Joe turned back to the sink and pulled out the plug. He stood watching the soapy water drain slowly away, letting the relief wash over him – he'd managed to get rid of another undead pet. Though he still had to face the coach trip home – where he knew Matt would have more questions for him! Joe sighed. He still wasn't sure whether to tell Matt the truth.

UNDEAD PETS

He was just about to leave the kitchen when he heard a low rumbling from the plughole. Followed by a horrible gurgling noise…

Joe raised his eyebrows. Bad plumbing? Blocked pipes?

"JOOOOOOOEEEEEE?" ARE YOU THERE, JOOOOEEEEEE?" called a bubbly voice from deep down within the plughole. "I NEEED YOOUR HELLP!"

OUT NOW!

SAM HAY

UNDEAD PETS

RETURN OF THE HUNGRY HAMSTER

Joe is just an ordinary boy until he makes a wish on a spooky Egyptian amulet...

Now he's the Protector of UNDEAD PETS ... and there's a ravenous rodent on the rampage!

Dumpling the hamster got sucked up a vacuum cleaner. Can Joe help him sort out his unfinished business, so he can finally bite the dust?

OUT NOW!

Joe is just an ordinary boy
until he makes a wish on a
spooky Egyptian amulet...

Now he's the Protector of
UNDEAD PETS ... and there's
a crazy cat on his tail!

Poor Pickle met her end under the wheels of a car.
Can Joe help Pickle protect her sister before
there's another cat-astrophe?

Joe is just an ordinary boy
until he makes a wish on a
spooky Egyptian amulet...

Now he's the Protector of
UNDEAD PETS ... and there's a
ghoulish goldfish making a splash!

Fizz the goldfish got flushed.
Can Joe help him take revenge so
he can go belly up forever?

MEET
the characters!

ENTER
the competition!

www.undeadpets.co.uk

PLAY
the game!

WATCH
the trailer